A Yom Tov Book of Poems

Tishrei Tales

By Reuven Bauman

Illustrated by Sarah Zee

MENUCHA PUBLISHERS

Menucha Publishers, Inc.
© 2019 by Tzivia Bauman
Typeset and designed by the Virtual Paintbrush
All rights reserved

ISBN 978-1-61465-799-6

Published and distributed by:
Menucha Publishers, Inc.
1235 38th Street
Brooklyn, NY 11218
Tel/Fax: 718-232-0856
www.menuchapublishers.com
sales@menuchapublishers.com

Printed in China

In Memory of

Rabbi Reuven Bauman

Reuven Tzvi *z"l*
ben Menachem Yitzchak

*A devoted and beloved teacher
who left an enduring impact
on the many lives he touched.*

Contents

Editor's Note

On April 16, 2019, I received the following e-mail from Rabbi Bauman.

> Hello, this is a book of yom tov poems, geared toward second to fourth graders, although children both older and younger will enjoy them as well. The book itself, as well as some of the poems, is not yet titled. Please let me know if you can publish it. Thanks!
> Reuven Bauman

I wrote him back that Menucha does not publish poetry. His response on May 1st was as follows:

> Okay, thanks. Can you just explain why not? I tried sending them to magazines, and they also said they don't print poetry. What's wrong with poetry?

What is wrong with poetry? I thought that was a great question. Other than the fact that poetry doesn't sell well, I couldn't think of a proper response. And although I lost my opportunity to give Rabbi Bauman an answer, I will attempt to answer his question now.

Poetry is the language of the heart and it can often communicate more directly and honestly than prose. It often holds multiple layers of meaning hidden within its rhythmic and harmonious lines.

So I would like to rephrase Rabbi Bauman's question a bit. Instead of asking what's wrong with poetry, I'd like to ask, what's wrong with us that we don't want to read poetry?

Rabbi Bauman's book of poems is intended to give children stories they can identify with that show the reward that mitzvos and davening can bring. Of course in the real world we do not always see the results that we hoped for. But in this book, the children's young and sensitive hearts are protected. They can identify with the characters and enjoy the happy endings.

Although this book contains stories in verse for children about Rosh Hashanah, Yom Kippur, and Sukkos, there is hidden meaning revealed in these poems as well.

While re-reading the poem about Yom Kippur, I was startled to read the following verses:

Life's not always easy,
You must put in your best effort,
And doing the right thing,
Well, sometimes it might hurt.

I hope you're ready too,
More prepared than you were before,
To do all of Hashem's mitzvos,
No matter what's in store.

Who could imagine that like the lines of his own verse, Rabbi Bauman put in his best effort to do a mitzvah, not knowing what was in store for him? And as he himself reminds us: life is not always easy.

Rabbi Bauman, I'm sorry I didn't answer the question in your last e-mail to me. But, I can say now: no, there is nothing wrong with poetry. And yes, we will publish your poems.

We sincerely hope that this book of poems will provide meaning and comfort to everyone who was touched by Rabbi Bauman during his short, yet impactful time in this world.

Esther Heller

Rosh Hashanah

A Sticky Sweet New Year

Summer vacation is over,
Fall is finally here.
Camp is but a memory
As we start a brand-new year.

The leaves have changed their colors,
The weather has turned cool.
The kids are wearing jackets
As they all walk home from school.

"I wish it was still summer,"
Complains Yossel Begun,
"Hot days for play and swimming,
Each day *so* full of fun.

"And now it's work, work, work,
At home and then at school,
A ton of tests and quizzes
And following every rule.

"I can't seem to be happy
Even when I try,
There's nothing to look forward to,"
He says with a big sigh.

"How can you say that?
What do you mean?!
I'm so very excited!"
Says his friend Sruly Green.

"In just one more week
Rosh Hashanah will come,
With shofars and apples
And honey, so yum!"

"You're right," answers Yossel,
Beginning to smile,
The first time he's done so
In quite a long while.

"But are honey and apples
Really that great?
So very exciting,
You really can't wait?"

"Well, you see," Sruly begins,
"You might find this funny,
But my most favorite food
Is any food with honey!

"The taste is so delicious!
It is so very sweet!
It's better still than candy,
It's my most favorite treat!

"I really cannot wait
For Rosh Hashanah night.
That's when I turn my *seudah*
Into a sweet honey delight!

"I drip a lot of honey
On everything I eat,
So all my tasty food
Is also very sweet!

"I squeeze lots on my challah
Till the whole big piece is smothered,
Then I dip an apple in it
Till the entire fruit is covered.

"My gefilte fish goes swimming
In a gooey, honey sea,
Then it's on to honeyed chicken soup;
Yummy, you must agree.

"For the main dish I compose
A new song for all to hear,
'Dip the brisket in the honey,
Have a happy sweet new year!'

"For dessert it's honey cookies
Along with honey pie,
And honey-flavored ice cream,
You'll love it, give a try!

"By the time that I am finished
With my honey-flavored meal,
My hands are very sticky,
My lips are glued and sealed.

"The more honey the better,
It's more than just a treat.
It's our way of asking Hashem
For a year that's just as sweet."

On Rosh Hashanah morning
It's packed inside the shul.
The kids are davening nicely
Just like they learned in school.

All are now awaiting
The shofar blasts to sound.
Reb Yankel Roth's the *ba'al tokea*,
The very best around.

His *tekios* are the clearest,
He never makes mistakes,
He never has to stop for breath,
He doesn't shake or quake.

His famous *tekiah gedolah*
Is nearly a full minute.
If there would be a shofar contest
He would surely win it.

When anybody asks him
How he knows to blow so well,
With a twinkle in his eye,
Here's the story that he'll tell.

"My great-great Zeidy Velvel
From the city of Barnea
Was famous in his city
As a master *ba'al tokea*.

"His instrument was passed
From Zeidy Velvel to his son.
For many generations,
Our family's used this one.

"It is very sentimental,
To me the shofar's priceless.
If it would break or get lost
It would be an awful crisis!

"This is the only shofar
That I have ever known,
This is the only shofar
That I have ever blown.

"So that's my little secret,
Why my blasts all sound so good.
My special shofar makes me sound
Even better than I should."

Reb Yankel is all ready,
Not a single tiny noise
Is heard inside the shul,
From all the little girls and boys.

But as Reb Yankel reaches
To take the shofar in his palm,
Something awful happens
That breaks the quiet calm!

His beloved shofar slips,
It falls right from his hand!
We all look on in horror
As we watch his shofar land.

The fragile shofar falls
Onto the floor with a loud crash!
Everybody hears the crack
And sees the narrow gash.

Reb Yankel looks so very sad,
His face is filled with pain
That his beloved shofar
Will never be the same.

He starts with a whimper,
Then he gives a long, loud sigh.
Reb Yankel the *ba'al tokea*
Just stands in place and cries.

No one knows what to do next,
Not even the old Rav.
Everyone just davens for
Help from the One Above.

But then, from the back of the shul,
A young boy can be seen,
Slowly coming toward the bimah—
It is little Sruly Green!

He walks up to the bimah steps,
His face all scrunched and nervous.
He says to Reb Yankel Roth,
"Can I please be of service?"

He takes the shofar in his hand
And then he grows quite calm
As he begins to rub the shofar
Between his two small palms.

He starts with his right hand:
He wipes it and he scrubs it,
Then moves it to his left hand,
Where he rubs and rubs and rubs it.

His hands are doused in honey
Which he uses to fill the crack
And soon the gash is nearly sealed;
They'll get their shofar back!

But then the honey starts dripping
Through the shofar's hole.
He thought he's fixed the problem
But he hasn't reached his goal.

Then suddenly a voice calls out,
"Please rest your tired muscle.
I think that I can help you out."
It is his best friend, Yossel!

"You're the one who told me
Rosh Hashanah's really fun,
A sweet and sticky holiday,"
Says Yossel Begun.

He helps his friend to spread the honey
That they had used as glue,
All over the cracked shofar,
Till it looks brand new.

Reb Yankel takes the shofar
That no longer has a rip.
He says the *berachos* loud and clear
And puts it to his lips.

Author's note:
If you've learned *Mishnayos Rosh Hashanah* in school,
You know that a cracked shofar is *passul.*
The *Mishnah Berurah paskens* that you may glue the shofar
But no one has *paskened* about honey so far!

He takes a deep long breath
And from the shofar there comes forth,
The most amazing *tekiah*
By the great Reb Yankel Roth!

The sound is so, so sweet,
Even nicer than before,
And it keeps on getting sweeter
As he continues blowing more.

It sounds just like honey,
Flowing sweet and pure.
It ascends straight to Heaven,
Of that they all are sure.

Then he faces the two "honey fixers"
And thanks them both so much.
He tells them they should always have
A sweet and sticky touch.

This year they all are written
Way up in Shamayim,
In Hashem's book of good life,
In Hashem's *sefer hachaim*.

For a year so full of *nachas*,
For a year so full of health,
Of *yeshuos*, of *nechamos*,
For a year so full of wealth.

And may we too be inscribed
On Hashem's sweet, special list
For a year that's full of sweetness,
For a year that can't be missed!

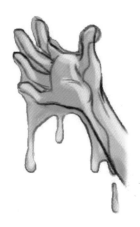

Yom Kippur

The Mitzvah Watch

Hello everybody,
My name's Leibel Levov,
I have just turned bar mitzvah—
I get a big, big mazel tov!

I remember the words
Of my great-uncle Yehuda,
That he said very nicely
At my bar mitzvah *seudah*:

"Life's not always easy,
You must put in your best effort,
And doing the right thing,
Well, sometimes it might hurt.

"Learn Torah and do *chesed*,
Do mitzvos every day!
Grow in *yiras Shamayim*,
That's all I have to say."

Well, today is Yom Kippur,
The great Day of Atonement,
A great day for commitment,
To do mitzvos every moment.

I'm standing here in shul
With my brother and my dad,
But this is the hardest Yom Kippur
That I have ever had.

In the past I have enjoyed it,
I've always been inspired.
But this year I'm just hungry,
I'm thirsty and I'm tired.

This is the first Yom Kippur
That I really have to fast.
It's really not so easy,
I'm not sure I can last.

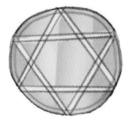

The davening is so long,
I'm not sure I can take it.
This mitzvah's very hard,
I don't think that I'll make it.

Maybe a short, quick break
Together with my brother
Will help to keep me going,
One way or another.

"Leibel?" my brother asks me,
"Do you remember what we used to do
Every Yom Kippur davening
Since the age of two?

"When everyone in shul
Would bow down to the ground
We'd bow down right beside them,
And then we'd look around.

"And all that we could see
Were tons of Yom Kippur crocs
And lots of canvas sneakers
And feet just wearing socks!

"Remember when old Hymie
Put his head down on the floor?
And fell so fast asleep
That he gave a little snore?"

I answer, "I remember
That part of the service,
But this year all that bowing
Is making me so nervous.

"I feel so very weak
Since I've had nothing to eat,
If I bow down I'm scared
I won't get back up on my feet!"

And that is when I notice
My empty, bare right arm.
"I'm missing my new watch!"
I yell out in alarm.

"My new bar mitzvah watch!
So expensive, sentimental!
The present that I got from
Uncle Izzie and Aunt Yentel!"

I'm so very upset,
I just cannot believe it!
I really have to find it,
I just have to retrieve it!

We start looking around,
My brother and I,
But we just can't find it;
I think I'll start to cry!

I go back into shul,
Weak and upset.
I try to daven, but that watch—
Is too hard to forget.

Well, soon it's *kor'im* time
And everyone gets ready
To bow down on the floor,
But I feel so unsteady.

I feel way too weak
And also upset
Because of a watch
I just can't forget.

Then I remember Uncle's speech
At my bar mitzvah celebration,
About keeping all the mitzvos
With total dedication.

"Life's not always easy,
You must put in your best effort,
And doing the right thing,
Well, sometimes it might hurt.

"Learn Torah and do *chesed*,
Do mitzvos every day!
Grow in *yiras Shamayim*,"
That's what he had to say.

And today on Yom Kippur,
The Day of Atonement,
It's a day for commitment
To do mitzvos every moment.

So I decide to do it
Even though I feel *so* sick,
I'll just bend and bow down,
Then get up really quick.

So I bow down real low
With my face to the ground,
Like when we were younger,
I look all around.

And all that I can see
Are tons of Yom Kippur crocs
And lots of canvas sneakers
And feet just wearing socks!

And there is good old Hymie
With his head down on the floor,
He's fallen fast asleep,
He gives a little snore.

I start to get up,
So proud of my decision,
When I see something glinting
In my peripheral vision.

I quickly crawl right over,
Not daring to breathe.
Could it be my lost watch,
I am about to retrieve?

I come near and look,
It is shiny and gold.
My watch! I have found it!
Lo and behold!

If I would not have bowed
All the way to the ground,
It could be that my watch
Would not have been found.

By doing a mitzvah
You never, ever lose.
Instead, you are rewarded
For the mitzvah that you choose.

As I sit down in my seat
I feel so inspired.
I know that I will make it,
Though I am hungry and tired.

To fast and also daven
May not be very easy
But I know I can do it,
Though I'm still feeling queasy.

The rest of the Yom Kippur
Seems to fly right by.
When it ends I feel better,
I feel like I could fly.

Now indeed I feel ready
To do mitzvos every moment,
And on what better day,
Than the Day of Atonement?

I hope you're ready too,
More prepared than you were before,
To do all of Hashem's mitzvos,
No matter what's in store.

Sukkos

Sukkos in the Rain?

I sit down on the couch
And stare at the backyard,
Watching the rain fall
Steadily and hard.

I sigh a great big sigh,
I feel so downcast,
I ask myself out loud,
"How long will this rain last?"

It's been raining ever since
Last Tuesday afternoon,
And it doesn't seem as if
It will be letting up too soon.

The whole backyard has turned
Into a giant muddy lake,
The sun does not want to give
Those dark rain clouds a break.

The squirrels won't leave the trees,
The butterflies won't flap their wings.
The birds don't want to chirp
And the frogs won't croak and sing.

I usually don't mind
When it rains a lot all year
But now I really need
For this rain to disappear.

The happy yom tov of Sukkos
Will be starting soon—tonight!
The nights must be all clear,
The days must shine so bright.

It seems it won't let up
Within the next few hours,
The weather forecast says
We should expect a lot of showers.

I love eating in the sukkah
When everyone is there,
Laughing with my family,
Enjoying the crisp air.

I love relaxing in our sukkah
On a yom tov afternoon,
Shmoozing with my friends
While we hum a yom tov tune.

But it doesn't really seem
Like I'm going to get my chance,
We won't be sitting in the sukkah
In this rainy circumstance.

What will really make me sad
If this rain continues falling,
Is that I'll feel just like that servant
Who hears his master calling:

"I am so very thirsty,
Can you please bring me a drink?
I would like some cold fresh water,
Please bring it from the sink."

But when the servant brings it
He's splashed right in his face!
His master sends him packing;
The servant feels disgraced.

"I do not want your service!"
Says the master with a glare.
"Don't try to do my bidding,
I really do not care."

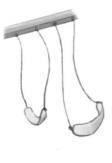

That's the way I'll feel
If Hashem won't stop this rain;
Like He doesn't want my mitzvah.
It would cause me so much pain.

Totty and my brother Baruch
Are preparing for the celebrations,
They're wearing boots and raincoats
And hanging decorations.

I snap up my raincoat
And put on my hood,
I zip up my rain boots
To stay as dry as I could.

I open my umbrella
And bravely step outside,
I slosh past the swing set
And glide past the slide.

I step into the sukkah,
Look up at the decorations.
They are drooping and gloomy
And I groan in frustration.

It seems everyone's excited,
Everyone but me.
But look at all those rain clouds!
How happy could I be?

I hold tight to my umbrella
And cry out to the others,
"What's the point?" I ask my father.
"Why bother?" I ask my brother.

"The happy yom tov of Sukkos
Will be starting soon—tonight!
The nights must be all clear,
The days must shine so bright!

"It seems like all this rain
Will continue to fall forever
And we will never have a chance
To sit in the sukkah together!

"We aren't even saying
The words *'mashiv haruach'*!
We still have another week,
According to the *luach*!"

Totty turns to me
And says with a knowing smile,
"I know, Shira, it's been raining
For quite a little while.

"I see that you are sad,
You're feeling so downcast.
I know that you are wondering,
How long will this rain last?

"But if you have an issue,
You do not need to kvetch!
There's something more effective;
A Tehillim you can fetch!

"You should daven to Hashem
And share your thoughts with Him!
Tefillah can always help you,
Even when things seem grim!

"Maybe Hashem's just waiting
To hear your heartfelt prayer,
Maybe you'll get the answer you want;
There's no need to despair!"

I'm standing in the rain,
It mixes with my tears.
I think about his words,
They help me with my fears.

It's true that it does seem
That the rain will never end,
And I won't have a chance
To enjoy the sukkah with my friends.

But I don't want to get
Water splashed onto my face
Or be sent away,
And leave in disgrace.

But my father's words make sense:
It is simple, just a fact,
That *tefillah* is the right way
For a good Jew to react.

So I slosh back inside
And go up to my room.
I already feel better,
With relief from my gloom.

I sit down on my bed
And I whisper so low,
Talking to Hashem,
Carefully and slow.

"Hashem, the yom tov of Sukkos
Will be here soon—tonight!
But the nights must be all clear,
The days must shine so bright!

"I love eating in the sukkah
When everyone is there,
Laughing with my family,
Enjoying the crisp air.

"I love relaxing in our sukkah
On a yom tov afternoon,
Shmoozing with my friends
While we hum a yom tov tune.

"But now it doesn't seem
Like I'm going to get my chance.
We can't sit in our sukkah
In this rainy circumstance.

"Hashem, you are the One
Who causes it to rain.
Maybe for this Sukkos,
You can cause it to refrain?

"I know that You hear me,
I know You may say 'No!'
But my wishes and my desires,
I would just like You to know."

When I'm all finished,
When my *tefillah* is all prayed,
I go over to my window
And I lift up the shade.

The sun is shining brightly,
The clouds have gone away!
The rain has stopped its raining,
It's a shiny, sunny day!

Although it is still muddy,
There's no more backyard lake.
The sun has finally given
Those dark rain clouds a break.

The squirrels climb down the trees,
The butterflies flap their wings.
The birds begin to chirp
As the frogs croak and sing.

What I see outside
Is simply unbelievable!
It's a true, real miracle,
It's simply inconceivable!

"Hashem has listened to me,
He has answered my prayer!
I see there was no reason
For me to despair!"

For the next seven days,
Starting that very night,
The weather is clear,
The days shine so bright.

We eat in the sukkah,
Everyone is there.
I laugh with my family,
Enjoying the crisp air.

I relax in the sukkah
All the yom tov afternoons,
Shmoozing with my friends
While we hum yom tov tunes.

I look up at the *sechach*,
Thinking of what I've learned.
If I ever need something,
To Hashem I'll simply turn.

If I ever have an issue,
I won't need to kvetch!
There is something more effective;
A Tehillim I will fetch!

I will just speak to Hashem
And share my thoughts with Him!
Tefillah can always help
Even when things seem grim!

Maybe Hashem was just waiting
To hear my heartfelt plea.
I know He'll always listen,
Whatever the answer might be.

About the Author

Rabbi Reuven Bauman was born in 1983, the second of twelve children. He grew up in Teaneck, New Jersey. He lived in Elizabeth, New Jersey; Savannah, Georgia; and most recently Norfolk, Virginia, where he was a beloved rebbe at Yeshivas Toras Chaim.

Rabbi Bauman was a devoted and beloved teacher. He had the ability to understand and reach out to children who do not feel inspired to learn. He knew how to connect with young students who are struggling. He left a profound impact on his students and all who came into contact with him.

Rabbi Bauman also authored *Yanky's Amazing Discovery* (Menucha Publishers, 2018), a book written with great empathy and sensitivity. His goal was to uplift and excite all children with stories about HaRav Yaakov Kamenetsky, *zt"l*. He wanted to show his readers how we can all learn from a *gadol* to become better people.

In Memory of Our Brother

If you were so fortunate
And happened to meet
Our brother, Reuven, *z"l*,
Out on the street,

The first thing you'd notice
And sensation you'd feel
Was his wide and bright smile
And his *simchah* so real.

And then, you'd be caught
By the warmth of his eyes,
A peek into his depth,
So caring, so wise.

To each different person
He knew what to say.
And for each individual
Just how, in what way.

Then in his simple,
unassuming way,
He'd say just the thing
To add sheen to your day.

And if you were luckier yet
And had a real talk,
You'd get a small glimpse
Of the path he did walk.

And in those few minutes
You'd get a fair share
Of his positive humor
And *hashkafah*, so clear.

He excelled at relationships,
A giver par excellence,
Put everyone else
Before his own needs and wants.

A master of balance—
Everything in right measure.
The right time for what,
It all was a pleasure.

If you were so fortunate
And happened to see
Our brother, Reuven,
At home with family,

You'd get a good lesson
On what true *chinuch* is,
You'd see his excitement
And love for his kids.

With pictures of *gedolim*
Covering the walls,
And Hashem's beautiful nature
Adorning the halls.

The fridge is all plastered
With smiles on faces
Of family and friends
From all different places.

A *makom Torah*,
That was his place.
You could feel it and see it
In every corner and space.

He kept his focus
With constant ascension,
An *eved Hashem*
Without commotion or attention.

Reuven, dear brother,
You've shown us the way.
You will still keep on guiding us:
"What will Reuven say?"

Your pleasantness, sweetness,
With true *ahavas Yisrael*
Are areas we strive for
And we'll try to excel.

Your thirst for Torah,
Your *emes*, your *gevurah*, such might,
We look up to them
As our guiding light.

We are davening and know
It won't be too long
Before we all dance together
With *simchah* and song,

With the coming of
The ultimate *yeshuah*
When Hashem reveals all good
With the final *Geulah*.

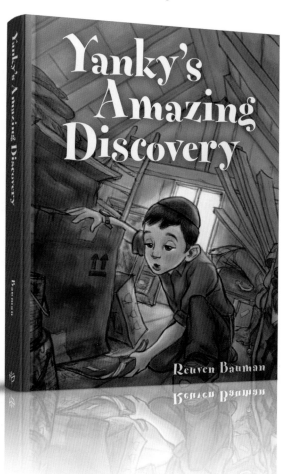